Charles McRae

Fathers of biology

Charles McRae

Fathers of biology

ISBN/EAN: 9783337214937

Printed in Europe, USA, Canada, Australia, Japan

Cover: Foto ©Andreas Hilbeck / pixelio.de

More available books at **www.hansebooks.com**

FATHERS OF BIOLOGY

BY

CHARLES McRAE, M.A., F.L.S.

FORMERLY SCHOLAR OF EXETER COLLEGE, OXFORD

PERCIVAL & CO.

KING STREET, COVENT GARDEN

London

1890

PREFACE.

IT is hoped that the account given, in the following pages, of the lives of five great naturalists may not be found devoid of interest. The work of each one of them marked a definite advance in the science of Biology.

There is often among students of anatomy and physiology a tendency to imagine that the facts with which they are now being made familiar have all been established by recent observation and experiment. But even the slight knowledge of the history of Biology, which may be obtained from a perusal of this little book, will show that, so far from such being the case, this branch of science is of venerable antiquity. And, further, if in the place of this misconception a desire is aroused in the reader for a fuller acquaintance with the writings of the early anatomists the chief aim of the author will have been fulfilled.

CONTENTS.

		PAGE
HIPPOCRATES	.. ..	1
ARISTOTLE	.. ..	19
GALEN	... .	45
VESALIUS	.. ..	63
HARVEY	.. ..	83

HIPPOCRATES.

HIPPOCRATES.

OWING to the lapse of centuries, very little is known with certainty of the life of Hippocrates, who was called with affectionate veneration by his successors "the divine old man," and who has been justly known to posterity as "the Father of Medicine."

He was probably born about 470 B.C., and, according to all accounts, appears to have reached the advanced age of ninety years or more. He must, therefore, have lived during a period of Greek history which was characterized by great intellectual activity; for he had, as his contemporaries, Pericles the famous statesman; the poets Æschylus, Sophocles, Euripides, Aristophanes, and Pindar; the philosopher Socrates, with his disciples Xenophon and Plato; the historians Herodotus and Thucydides; and Phidias the unrivalled sculptor.

In the island of Cos, where he was born, stood one of the most celebrated of the temples of Æsculapius, and in this temple—because he was descended from the Asclepiadæ—Hippocrates inherited from his forefathers

an important position. Among the Asclepiads the habit
of physical observation, and even manual training in
dissection, were imparted traditionally from father to
son from the earliest years, thus serving as a preparation
for medical practice when there were no written treatises
to study.[1]

Although Hippocrates at first studied medicine under
his father, he had afterwards for his teachers Gorgias and
Democritus, both of classic fame, and Herodicus, who is
known as the first person who applied gymnastic exercises
to the cure of diseases.

The Asclepions, or temples of health, were erected
in various parts of Greece as receptacles for invalids,
who were in the habit of resorting to them to seek the
assistance of the god. These temples were mostly
situated in the neighbourhood of medicinal springs, and
each devotee at his entrance was made to undergo a
regular course of bathing and purification. Probably
his diet was also carefully attended to, and at the
same time his imagination was worked upon by music
and religious ceremonies. On his departure, the restored patient usually showed his gratitude by presenting
to the temple votive tablets setting forth the circumstances of his peculiar case. The value of these to men
about to enter on medical studies can be readily understood; and it was to such treasures of recorded obser-

[1] Grote's "Aristotle," vol. i. p. 3.

vations — collected during several generations — that Hippocrates had access from the commencement of his career.

Owing to the peculiar constitution of the Asclepions, medical and priestly pursuits had, before the time of Hippocrates, become combined; and, consequently, although rational means were to a certain extent applied to the cure of diseases, the more common practice was to resort chiefly to superstitious modes of working upon the imagination. It is not surprising, therefore, to find that every sickness, especially epidemics and plagues, were attributed to the anger of some offended god, and that penance and supplications often took the place of personal and domestic cleanliness, fresh air, and light.

It was Hippocrates who emancipated medicine from the thraldom of superstition, and in this way wrested the practice of his art from the monopoly of the priests. In his treatise on " The Sacred Disease " (possibly epilepsy), he discusses the controverted question whether or not this disease was an infliction from the gods; and he decidedly maintains that there is no such a thing as a sacred disease, for all diseases arise from natural causes, and no one can be ascribed to the gods more than another. He points out that it is simply because this disease is unlike other diseases that men have come to regard its cause as divine, and yet it is not really more wonderful than the paroxysms of fevers and many other diseases not thought sacred. He exposes the cunning of the impostors who pretend to cure men by purifications and spells; "who give themselves out as being excessively religious, and as knowing more than other people;" and he argues that "whoever is able, by purifications and conjurings, to drive away such an affection, will be able, by other practices, to excite it, and, according to this view, its divine nature is entirely done away with." "Neither, truly," he continues, "do I count it a worthy opinion to hold that the body of a man is polluted by the divinity, the most impure by the most holy; for, were it defiled, or did it suffer from any other thing, it would be like to be purified and sanctified rather than polluted by the divinity." As an additional argument against the cause being divine, he adduces the fact that this disease is hereditary, like other diseases, and that it attacks persons of a peculiar temperament, namely, the phlegmatic, but not the bilious; and "yet if it were really more divine than the others," he justly adds, "it ought to befall all alike."

Again, speaking of a disease common among the Scythians, Hippocrates remarks that the people attributed it to a god, but that "to me it appears that such affections are just as much divine as all others are, and that no one disease is either more divine or more human than another, but that all are alike divine, for that each has its own nature, and that no one arises without a natural cause."

From this it will be seen that Hippocrates regarded all phenomena as at once divine and scientifically determinable. In this respect it is interesting to compare him with one of his most illustrious contemporaries, namely, with Socrates, who distributed phenomena into two classes: one wherein the connection of antecedent and consequent was invariable and ascertainable by human study, and wherein therefore future results were accessible to a well-instructed foresight; the other, which the gods had reserved for themselves and their unconditional agency, wherein there was no invariable or ascertainable sequence, and where the result could only be foreknown by some omen or prophecy, or other special inspired communication from themselves. Each of these classes was essentially distinct, and required to be looked at and dealt with in a manner radically incompatible with the other. Physics and astronomy, in the opinion of Socrates, belonged to the divine class of phenomena in which human research was insane, fruitless, and impious.[1]

Hippocrates divided the causes of diseases into two classes : the one comprehending the influence of seasons, climates, water, situation, and the like; the other consisting of such causes as the amount and kind of food and exercise in which each individual indulges. He

[1] Grote's " History of Greece," vol. i. p. 358.

considered that while heat and cold, moisture and dry-
ness, succeeded one another throughout the year, the
human body underwent certain analogous changes which
influenced the diseases of the period. With regard to
the second class of causes producing diseases, he attributed many disorders to a vicious system of diet, for
excessive and defective diet he considered to be equally
injurious.

In his medical doctrines Hippocrates starts with the
axiom that the body is composed of the four elements
—air, earth, fire, and water. From these the four fluids
or humours (namely, blood, phlegm, yellow bile, and
black bile) are formed. Health is the result of a right
condition and proper proportion of these humours,
disease being due to changes in their quality or distribution. Thus inflammation is regarded as the passing of
blood into parts not previously containing it. In the
course of a disorder proceeding favourably, these humours
undergo spontaneous changes in quality. This process
is spoken of as *coction*, and is the sign of returning health,
as preparing the way for the expulsion of the morbid
matters—a state described as the *crisis*. These crises
have a tendency to occur at certain periods, which are
hence called *critical days*. As the critical days answer to
the periods of the process of coction, they are to be
watched with anxiety, and the actual condition of the
patient at these times is to be compared with the state

which it was expected he ought to show. From these observations the physician may predict the course which the remainder of the disease will probably take, and derive suggestions as to the practice to be followed in order to assist Nature in her operations.

Hippocrates thus appears to have studied "the natural history of diseases." As stated above, his practice was to watch the manner in which the humours were undergoing their fermenting coction, the phenomena displayed in the critical days, and the aspect and nature of the critical discharges—not to attempt to check the process going on, but simply to assist the natural operation. His principles and practice were based on the theory of the existence of a restoring essence (or φύσις) penetrating through all creation; the agent which is constantly striving to preserve all things in their natural state, and to restore them when they are preternaturally deranged. In the management of this *vis medicatrix naturæ* the art of the physician consisted. Attention, therefore, to regimen and diet was the principal remedy Hippocrates employed; nevertheless he did not hesitate, when he considered that occasion required, to administer such a powerful drug as hellebore in large doses.

The writings which are extant under the name of Hippocrates cannot all be ascribed to him. Many were doubtless written by his family, his descendants, or his pupils. Others are productions of the Alexandrian school, some of these being considered by critics as wilful forgeries, the high prices paid by the Ptolemies for books of reputation probably having acted as inducements to such fraud. The following works have generally been admitted as genuine :—

1. On Airs, Waters, and Places.
2. On Ancient Medicine.
3. On the Prognostics.
4. On the Treatment in Acute Diseases.
5. On Epidemics [Books I. and III.].
6. On Wounds of the Head.
7. On the Articulations.
8. On Fractures.
9. On the Instruments of Reduction.
10. The Aphorisms [Seven Books].
11. The Oath.

The works "On Fractures," "On the Articulations," "On Injuries to the Head," and "On the Instruments of Reduction," deal with anatomical or surgical matters, and exhibit a remarkable knowledge of osteology and anatomy generally. It has sometimes been doubted if Hippocrates could ever have had opportunities of gaining this knowledge from dissections of the human body, for it has been thought that the feeling of the age was diametrically opposed to such a practice, and that Hippocrates would not have dared to violate this feeling. The language used, however, in some passages in the work

"On the Articulations," seems to put the matter beyond doubt. Thus he says in one place, "But if one will strip the point of the shoulder of the fleshy parts, and where the muscle extends, and also lay bare the tendon that goes from the armpit and clavicle to the breast," etc. And again, further on in the same treatise, "It is evident, then, that such a case could not be reduced either by succussion or by any other method, unless one were to cut open the patient, and then, having introduced the hand into one of the great cavities, were to push outwards from within, which one might do in the dead body, but not at all in the living."

His descriptions of the vertebræ, with all their processes and ligaments, as well as his account of the general characters of the internal viscera, would not have been as free from error as they are if he had derived all his knowledge from the dissection of the inferior animals. Moreover, it is indisputable that, within less than a hundred years from the death of Hippocrates, the human body was openly dissected in the schools of Alexandria— nay, further, that even the vivisection of condemned criminals was not uncommon. It would be unreasonable to suppose that such a practice as the former sprang up suddenly under the Ptolemies, and it seems, therefore, highly probable that it was known and tolerated in the time of Hippocrates. It is not surprising, when we remember the rude appliances and methods which then obtained, that in his knowledge of minute anatomy Hippocrates should compare unfavourably with anatomists of the present day. Of histology, and such other subjects as could not be brought within his direct personal observation, the knowledge of Hippocrates was necessarily defective. Thus he wrote of the tissues without distinguishing them; confusing arteries, veins, and nerves, and speaking of muscles vaguely as "flesh." But with matters within the reach of the Ancient Physician's own careful observation, the case is very different. This is well shown in his wonderful chapter on the club-foot, in which he not only states correctly the true nature of the malformation, but gives some very sensible directions for rectifying the deformity in early life.

When human strength was not sufficient to restore a displaced limb, he skilfully availed himself of all the mechanical powers which were then known. He does not appear to have been acquainted with the use of pulleys for the purpose, but the axles which he describes as being attached to the bench which bears his name (*Scamnum Hippocratis*) must have been quite capable of exercising the force required.

The work called "'The Aphorisms," which was probably written in the old age of Hippocrates, consists of more than four hundred short pithy sentences, setting forth the principles of medicine, physiology, and natural philosophy. A large number of these sentences are evidently taken from the author's other works, especially those "On Air," etc., "On Prognostics," and "On the Articulations." They embody the result of a vast amount of observation and reflection, and the majority of them have been confirmed by the experience of two thousand years. A proof of the high esteem in which they have always been held is furnished by the fact that they have been translated into all the languages of the civilized world; among others, into Hebrew, Arabic, Latin, English, Dutch, Italian, German, and French. The following are a few examples of these aphorisms :—

"Spontaneous lassitude indicates disease."

"Old people on the whole have fewer complaints than the young; but those chronic diseases which do befall them generally never leave them."

"Persons who have sudden and violent attacks of fainting without any obvious cause die suddenly."

"Of the constitutions of the year, the dry upon the whole are more healthy than the rainy, and attended with less mortality."

"Phthisis most commonly occurs between the ages of eighteen and thirty-five years."

"If one give to a person in fever the same food which is given to a person in good health, what is strength to the one is disease to the other."

"Such food as is most grateful, though not so wholesome, is to be preferred to that which is better, but distasteful."

" Life is short and the art long; the opportunity fleeting; experience fallacious and judgment difficult. The physician must not only do his duty himself, but must also make the patient, the attendants and the externals, co-operate."

Hippocrates appears to have travelled a great deal, and to have practised his art in many places far distant from his native island. A few traditions of what he did during his long life remain, but differences of opinion exist as to the truth of these stories.

Thus one story says that when Perdiccas, the King of Macedonia, was supposed to be dying of consumption, Hippocrates discovered the disorder to be love-sickness, and speedily effected a cure. The details of this story scarcely seem to be worthy of credence, more especially as similar legends have been told of entirely different persons belonging to widely different times. There are, however, some reasons for believing that Hippocrates visited the Macedonian court in the exercise of his professional duties, for he mentions in the course of his writings, among places which he had visited, several which were situated in Macedonia; and, further, his son Thessalus appears to have afterwards been court physician to Archelaus, King of Macedonia.

Another story connects the name of Hippocrates with

the Great Plague which occurred at Athens in the time
of the Peloponnesian war. It is said that Hippocrates
advised the lighting of great fires with wood of some
aromatic kind, probably some species of pine. These,
being kindled all about the city, stayed the progress of
the pestilence. Others besides Hippocrates are, however, famous for having successfully adopted this practice.

A third legend states that the King of Persia, pur-
suing the plan (which in the two celebrated instances of
Themistocles and Pausanias had proved successful)
of attracting to his side the most distinguished persons
in Greece, wrote to Hippocrates asking him to pay
a visit to his court, and that Hippocrates refused to go.
Although the story is discarded by many scholars, it is
worthy of note that Ctesias, a kinsman and contemporary of Hippocrates, is mentioned by Xenophon in
the "Anabasis" as being in the service of the King of
Persia. And, with regard to the refusal of the venerable
physician to comply with the king's request, one cannot
lose sight of the fact that such refusal was the only
course consistent with the opinions he professed of
a monarchical form of government.

After his various travels Hippocrates, as seems to be
pretty generally admitted, spent the latter portion of his
life in Thessaly, and died at Larissa at a very advanced age.

It is difficult to speak of the skill and painstaking
perseverance of Hippocrates in terms which shall not

appear exaggerated and extravagant. His method of
cultivating medicine was in the true spirit of the
inductive philosophy. His descriptions were all derived from careful observation of its phenomena, and,
as a result, the greater number of his deductions have
stood unscathed the test of twenty centuries.

Still more difficult is it to speak with moderation of
the candour which impelled Hippocrates to confess
errors into which in his earlier practice he had fallen;
or of that freedom from superstition which entitled
him to be spoken of as a man who knew not how to
deceive or be deceived (" qui tam fallere quam falli
nescit "); or, lastly, of that purity of character and true
nobility of soul which are brought so distinctly to light
in the words of the oath translated below :—

" I swear by Apollo the Physician and Æsculapius,
and I call Hygeia and Panacea and all the gods and
goddesses to witness, that to the best of my power and
judgment I will keep this oath and this contract; to wit
—to hold him, who taught me this Art, equally dear to
me as my parents; to share my substance with him;
to supply him if he is in need of the necessaries of life;
to regard his offspring in the same light as my own
brothers, and to teach them this Art, if they shall desire
to learn it, without fee or contract; to impart the pre-
cepts, the oral teaching, and all the rest of the instruction to my own sons, and to the sons of my teacher,

and to pupils who have been bound to me by contract, and who have been sworn according to the law of medicine.

" I will adopt that system of regimen which, according to my ability and judgment, I consider for the benefit of my patients, and will protect them from everything noxious and injurious. I will give no deadly medicine to any one, even if asked, nor will I give any such counsel, and similarly I will not give to a woman the means of procuring an abortion. With purity and with holiness I will pass my life and practise my art. . . . Into whatever houses I enter I will go into them for the benefit of the sick, keeping myself aloof from every voluntary act of injustice and corruption and lust. Whatever in the course of my professional practice, or outside of it, I see or hear which ought not to be spread abroad, I will not divulge, as reckoning that all such should be kept secret. If I continue to observe this oath and to keep it inviolate, may it be mine to enjoy life and the practice of the Art respected among all men for ever. But should I violate this oath and forswear myself, may the reverse be my lot."

ARISTOTLE.

ARISTOTLE.

ABOUT the time that Hippocrates died, Aristotle, who may be regarded as the founder of the science of "Natural History," was born (B.C. 384) in Stagira, an unimportant Hellenic colony in Thrace, near the Macedonian frontier. His father was a distinguished physician, and, like Hippocrates, boasted descent from the Asclepiadæ. The importance attached by the Asclepiads to the habit of physical observation, which has been already referred to in the life of Hippocrates, secured for Aristotle, from his earliest years, that familiarity with biological studies which is so clearly evident in many of his works.

Both parents of Aristotle died when their son was still a youth, and in consequence of this he went to reside with Proxenus, a native of Atarneus, who had settled at Stagira. Subsequently he went to Athens and joined the school of Plato. Here he remained for about twenty years, and applied himself to study with such energy that he became pre-eminent even in that distinguished band of philosophers. He is said to have been spoken of by Plato as "the intellect" of the school, and to have been compared by him to a spirited colt that required the application of the rein to restrain its ardour.

Aristotle probably wrote at this time some philosophical works, the fame of which reached the ears of Philip, King of Macedonia, and added to the reputation which the young philosopher had already made with that monarch; for Philip is said to have written to him on the occasion of Alexander's birth, B.C. 356: "King Philip of Macedonia to Aristotle, greeting. Know that a son has been born to me. I thank the gods not so much that they have given him to me, as that they have permitted him to be born in the time of Aristotle. I hope that thou wilt form him to be a king worthy to succeed me and to rule the Macedonians."

After the death of Plato, which occurred in 347 B.C., Aristotle quitted Athens and went to Atarneus, where he stayed with Hermias, who was then despot of that town. Hermias was a remarkable man, who, from being a slave, had contrived to raise himself to the supreme power. He had been at Athens and had heard Plato's lectures, and had there formed a friendship for Aristotle. With this man the philosopher remained for three years, and was then compelled suddenly to seek refuge in Mitylene, owing to the perfidious murder of Hermias. The latter was decoyed out of the town by the Persian general, seized and sent prisoner to Artaxerxes, by whom he was hanged as a rebel. On leaving Atarneus, Aristotle took with him a niece of Hermias, named Pythias, whom he afterwards married. She died young, leaving an infant daughter.

Two or three years after this, Aristotle became tutor to Alexander, who was then about thirteen years old. The philosopher seems to have been a favourite with both the king and the prince, and, in gratitude for his services, Philip rebuilt Stagira and restored it to its former inhabitants, who had either been dispersed or carried into slavery. The king is said also to have established there a school for Aristotle. The high respect in which Alexander held his teacher is expressed in his saying that he honoured him no less than his own father, for while to one he owed life, to the other he owed all that made life valuable.

In 336 B.C. Alexander, who was then only about twenty years of age, became king, and Aristotle soon afterwards quitted Macedonia and took up his residence in Athens once more, after an absence of about twelve years. Here he opened a school in the Lycæum, a gymnasium on the eastern side of the city, and continued his work there for about twelve years, during which time Alexander was making his brilliant conquests. The lectures were given for the most part while walking in the garden, and in consequence, perhaps, of this, the sect received the name of the Peripatetics. The discourses were of two kinds—the *esoteric*, or abstruse, and the *exoteric*, or familiar; the former being delivered to the more advanced pupils only. During the greater part of this time Aristotle kept up correspondence with Alexander, who is said [1] to have placed at his disposal thousands of men, who were busily employed in collecting objects and in making observations for the completion of the philosopher's zoological researches. Alexander is, moreover, said to have given the philosopher eight hundred talents for the same purpose.

In spite of these marks of friendship and respect, Alexander, who was fast becoming intoxicated with success, and corrupted by Asiatic influences, gradually cooled in his attachment towards Aristotle. This may have been hastened by several causes, and among others by the freedom of speech and republican opinions of Callisthenes, a kinsman and disciple of Aristotle, who had been, by the latter's influence, appointed to attend on Alexander. Callisthenes proved so unpopular, that the king seems to have availed himself readily of the first plausible pretext for putting him to death, and to have threatened his former friend and teacher with a similar punishment. The latter, for his part, probably had a deep feeling of resentment towards the destroyer of his kinsman.

[1] Pliny, " Natural History," viii. c. 16.

Meanwhile the Athenians knew nothing of these altered relations between Aristotle and Alexander, but continued to regard the philosopher as thoroughly imbued with kingly notions (in spite of his writings being quite to the contrary); so that he was an object of suspicion and dislike to the Athenian patriots. Nevertheless, as long as Alexander was alive, Aristotle was safe from molestation. As soon, however, as Alexander's death became known, the anti-Macedonian feeling of the Athenians burst forth, and found a victim in the philosopher. A charge of impiety was brought against him. It was alleged that he had paid divine honours to his wife Pythias and to his friend Hermias. Now, for the latter, a eunuch, who from the rank of a slave had raised himself to the position of despot over a free Grecian community, so far from coupling his name (as Aristotle had done in his hymn) with the greatest personages of Hellenic mythology, the Athenian public felt that no contempt was too bitter. To escape the storm the philosopher retired to Chalcis, in Eubœa, then under garrison by Antipater, the Governor of Macedonia, remarking in a letter, written afterwards, that he did so in order that the Athenians might not have the opportunity of sinning a second time against philosophy (the allusion being, of course, to the fate of Socrates).

He probably intended to return to Athens again so

soon as the political troubles had abated, but in September, 322 B.C., he died at Chalcis. An overwrought mind, coupled with indigestion and weakness of the stomach, from which he had long suffered, was most probably the cause of death.   Some of his detractors, however, have asserted that he took poison, and others that he drowned himself in the Eubœan Euripus.

It is not easy to arrive at a just estimate of the character of Aristotle. By some of his successors he has been reproached with ingratitude to his teacher, Plato ; with servility to Macedonian power, and with love of costly display. How far these two last charges are due to personal slander it is impossible to say. The only ground for the first charge is, that he criticised adversely some of Plato's doctrines.

The manuscripts of Aristotle's works passed through many vicissitudes. At the death of the philosopher they were bequeathed to Theophrastus, who continued chief of the Peripatetic school for thirty-five years. Theophrastus left them, with his own works, to a philosophical friend and pupil, Neleus, who conveyed them from Athens to his residence at Scepsis, in Asia Minor. About thirty or forty years after the death of Theophrastus, the kings of Pergamus, to whom the city of Scepsis belonged, began collecting books to form a library on the Alexandrian plan. This led the heirs of Neleus to conceal their literary treasures in a cellar, and there the manuscripts remained for nearly a century and a half, exposed to injury from damp and worms. At length they were sold to Apellicon, a resident at Athens, who was attached to the Peripatetic sect. Many of the manuscripts were imperfect, having become worm-eaten or illegible. These defects Apellicon attempted to remedy; but, being a lover of books rather than a philosopher, he performed the work somewhat unskilfully. When Athens was taken by Sylla, 86 B.C., the library of Apellicon was transported to Rome. There various literary Greeks obtained access to it; and, among others, Tyrannion, a grammarian and friend of Cicero, did good service in the work of correction. Andronicus of Rhodes afterwards arranged the whole into sections, and published the manuscripts with a tabulated list.

The three principal works on biology which are extant are: "The History of Animals;" "On the Parts of Animals;" "On the Generation of Animals." The other biological works are: "On the Motion of Animals;" "On Respiration;" "Parva Naturalia;" — a series of essays which are planned to form an entire work on sense and the sensible.

"The History of Animals" is the largest and most important of Aristotle's works on biology. It contains a vast amount of information, not very methodically arranged, and spoiled by the occurrence here and there of very gross errors. It consists of nine books.

The first book opens with a division of the body into similar and dissimilar parts. Besides thus differing in their parts, animals also differ in their mode of life, their actions and dispositions. Thus some are aquatic, others terrestrial ; of the former, some breathe water, others air, and some neither. Of aquatic animals, some inhabit the sea, and others rivers, lakes, or marshes. Again, some animals are locomotive, and others are stationary. Some follow a leader, others act independently. Various differences are in this way pointed out, and there is no lack of illustration and detail, but a suspicion is excited that the generalizations are sometimes based upon insufficient facts. The book closes with a description of the different parts of the human body, both internal and external. In speaking of the ear, Aristotle seems to have been aware of what we now call the Eustachian tube, for he says, " There is no passage from the ear into the brain, but there is to the roof of the mouth." [1]

In the second book he passes on to describe the organs of animals. The animals are dealt with in groups —viviparous and oviparous quadrupeds, fish, serpents, birds, etc. The ape, elephant, chameleon, and some others are especially noticed.

The third book continues the description of the internal organs. References which are made to a diagram by letters, *a, b, c, d,* show that the work was originally

[1] " History of Animals," i. 11.

illustrated. At the close of this book Aristotle has some remarks on milk, and mentions the occasional appearance of milk in male animals. He speaks of a male goat at Lemnos which yielded so much that cakes of cheese were made from it. Similar instances of this phenomenon have been recorded by Humboldt, Burdach, Geoffroy St. Hilaire, and others.

In the first four chapters of the fourth book the anatomy of the invertebrata is dealt with, and the accounts given of certain mollusca and crustacea are very careful and minute. The rest of the book is devoted to a description of the organs of sense and voice; of sleep, and the distinctions of sex. The accurate knowledge which Aristotle exhibits of the anatomy and habits of marine animals, such as the Cephalopoda and the larger Crustacea, leaves no doubt that he derived it from actual observation. Professor Owen says, " Respecting the living habits of the Cephalopoda, Aristotle is more rich in detail than any other zoological author." What is now spoken of as the *hectocotylization* of one or more of the arms of the male cephalopod did not escape Aristotle's eye. And while he speaks of the teeth and that which serves these animals for a tongue, it is plain from the context that he means in the one case the two halves of the parrot-like beak, and in the other the anterior end of the odontophore.

Books five to seven deal with the subject of generation.

The eighth book contains a variety of details respecting animals, their food, migrations, hibernation, and diseases; with the influence of climate and locality upon them.

The ninth book describes the habits and instincts of animals. The details are interesting; but there is, as usual, very little attempt at classification. Disjointed statements and sudden digressions occur, the subjects being treated in the order in which they presented themselves to the author. Such curious statements as the following are met with : "The raven is an enemy to the bull and the ass, for it flies round them and strikes their eyes." " If a person takes a goat by the beard, all the rest of the herd stand by, as if infatuated, and look at it." " Female stags are captured by the sound of the pipe and by singing. When two persons go out to capture them, one shows himself, and either plays upon a pipe or sings, and the other strikes behind, when the first gives him the signal." " Swans have the power of song, especially when near the end of their life ; for they then fly out to sea, and some persons sailing near the coast of Libya have met many of them in the sea singing a mournful song, and have afterwards seen some of them die." " Of all wild animals, the elephant is the most tame and gentle ; for many of them are capable of instruction and intelligence, and they have been taught *to worship the king.*"

In the work "On the Parts of Animals," the author considers not only the phenomena of life exhibited by each species, but also the cause or causes to which these phenomena are attributable. After a general introduction, he proceeds to enumerate the three degrees of composition, viz. :—

(1) "Composition out of what some call the elements, such as air, earth, water, and fire," or "out of the elementary forces, hot and cold, solid and fluid, which form the material of all compound substances."

(2) Composition out of these primary substances of the homogeneous parts of animals, *e.g.* blood, fat, marrow, brain, flesh, and bone.

(3) Composition into the heterogeneous parts or organs. These parts he describes in detail, considering those belonging to sanguineous animals first and most fully.

These divisions correspond roughly to the threefold study of structure which we nowadays recognize as chemical, histological, and anatomical.

As examples of Aristotle's method of treatment, his descriptions of blood, the brain, the heart, and the lung may be considered.

Of the *blood* he says, "What are called fibres are found in the blood of some animals, but not of all. There are none, for instance, in the blood of deer and of roes, and for this reason the blood of such animals as these never coagulates. . . . Too great an excess of water makes animals timorous. . . . Such animals, on the other hand, as have thick and abundant fibres in their blood are of a more choleric temperament, and liable to bursts of passion. . . . Bulls and boars are choleric, for their blood is exceedingly rich in fibres, and the bull's, at any rate, coagulates more rapidly than that of any other animal. . . . If these fibres are taken out of the blood, the fluid that remains will no longer coagulate."

From these quotations it will be noted that Aristotle attributed the coagulum to the presence of fibres, and in this he anticipated Malpighi's discovery made in the seventeenth century. His remarks on the proportion of coagulum and serum in different animals, which is enlarged upon in the " History of Animals," [1] harmonize with modern observations. In another of his works [2] he remarks that the blood in certain diseased conditions will not coagulate. This is known to be the case in cholera, certain fevers, asphyxia, etc. ; and the fact was probably obtained from Hippocrates. Although Aristotle speaks here of entire absence of coagulation in the blood of the deer and the roe, in the " History of Animals " he admits an imperfect coagulation, for he says, " so that their blood does not coagulate like that of other animals." The animals named are commonly hunted, and it was

[1] Bk. iii. 19.   [2] " Meteorology," iv. 7–11.

probably after they had been hunted to death that he examined them. Now, it is generally admitted that coagulation under such circumstances is imperfect and even uncommon. The statement as to the richness in fibres of the blood of bulls and boars has been confirmed by some modern investigations, which have shown that the clot bears a proportion to the strength and ferocity of the animal. The remarks, however, as to the relative rapidity of coagulation would appear to be contradicted by later observations, for Thackrah came to the conclusion that coagulation commenced sooner in small and weak animals than in strong.

Of the *brain* Aristotle makes the following among other assertions : " Of all parts of the body there is none so cold as the brain. . . . Of all the fluids of the body it is the one that has the least blood, for, in fact, it has no blood at all in its proper substance. . . . That it has no continuity with the organs of sense is plain from simple inspection, and still more closely shown by the fact that when it is touched no sensation is produced. . . . The brain tempers the heat and seething of the heart. . . . In order that it may not itself be absolutely without heat, blood-vessels from the aorta end in the membrane which surrounds the brain. . . . Of all animals man has the largest brain in proportion to his size : and it is larger in men than in women. This is because the region of the heart and of the lung is hotter and richer in blood in man than in any other animal; and in men than in women. This again explains why man alone of animals stands erect. For the heat, overcoming any opposite inclination, makes growth take its own line of direction, which is from the centre of the body upwards. . . . Man again has more sutures in his skull than any other animal, and the male more than the female. The explanation is to be found in the greater size of the brain, which demands free ventilation proportionate to its bulk. . . . There is no brain in the hinder part of the head. . . . The brain in all animals that have one is placed in the front part of the head . . . because the heart, from which sensation proceeds, is in the front part of the body."

Although it would perhaps be difficult to find anywhere as many errors in as few words, yet it should be observed that Aristotle here shows himself to have been aware of the existence of the membranes of the brain—the *pia mater* and the *dura mater ;* and elsewhere [1] he says more explicitly, "Two membranes enclose the brain; that about the skull is the stronger; the inner membrane is slighter than the outer one." And further, it should be noted that he describes the latter membrane as a vascular one. The fact of the brain substance being insensible to mechanical irritation was known to Aristotle, and may have been learnt from the practice of Hippocrates.

[1] " History of Animals," i. 16.

Lastly, it should be remembered that—though this may have been but a lucky guess on Aristotle's part—the relative weight of brain to the entire body has been shown, with few exceptions, to be greater in man than in any other animal.

In describing the *heart* Aristotle says : " The heart lies about the centre of the body, but rather in its upper than in its lower half, and also more in front than behind. . . . In man it inclines a little towards the left, so that it may counterbalance the chilliness of that side. It is hollow, to serve for the reception of the blood; while its wall is thick, that it may serve to protect the source of heat. For here, and here alone, in all the viscera, and in fact in all the body, there is blood without blood-vessels, the blood elsewhere being always contained within vessels. The heart is the first of all the parts of the body to be formed, and no sooner is it formed than it contains blood. . . . For no sooner is the embryo formed than its heart is seen in motion like a living creature, and this before any of the other parts. The heart is abundantly supplied with sinews. . . . In no animal does the heart contain a bone, certainly in none of those that we ourselves have inspected, with the exception of the horse and a certain kind of ox. In animals of great size the heart has three cavities ; in smaller animals it has two ; and in all it has at least one."

It will be observed that here Aristotle so correctly describes the position of the human heart as to render it probable that he is speaking from actual inspection ; although man is not the only animal in which the heart is turned towards the left. In contrasting the heart with the other viscera he appears to have overlooked the existence of the coronary vessels, and to have imagined that the nutrition of the heart was effected directly by the blood in its cavities. Although the heart is not really the first part to appear, the observation of its very early appearance in the embryo, which he treats more fully elsewhere,[1] is alone enough to establish his reputation as an original observer. It is remarkable that Aristotle should have overlooked the presence of the valves of the heart, the structure and functions of which were fully investigated within thirty years of his death by the anatomists of the Alexandrian school. This is the more remarkable, as he calls attention here, and in the "History of Animals," to the sinews or tendons ($\nu\epsilon\hat{\upsilon}\rho\alpha$) with which, he says, the heart is supplied, and by which he probably meant chiefly the *chordæ tendineæ*. The "bone in the heart" of which he speaks was probably the cruciform ossification which is normally found in the ox and the stag below the origin of the aorta. It is found in the horse only in advanced age, or under abnormal conditions. The statement that the heart contains no more

[1] "History of Animals," vi. 3.

than three chambers has always been considered as a very gross blunder on the part of Aristotle. Even Cuvier, who generally lavishes upon the philosopher the most extravagant praise, sneers at this. Professor Huxley,[1] however, has shown, by a comparison of several passages from the " History of Animals," that what we now call the right auricle was regarded by the author as a venous sinus, as being a part not of the heart, but of the great vein (*i.e.* the superior and the inferior *venæ cavæ*).

Aristotle speaks of the *lung* as a single organ, subdivided, but having a common outlet—the trachea. Elsewhere [2] he says, " Canals from the heart pass to the lung and divide in the same fashion as the windpipe does, closely accompanying those from the windpipe through the whole lung." His theory of respiration, as explained in his treatise on the subject, is that it tempers the excessive heat produced in the heart. The lung is compared to a pair of bellows. When the lung is expanded, air rushes in; when it is contracted, the air is expelled. The heat from the heart causes the lung to expand—cold air rushes in, the heat is reduced, the lung collapses, and the air is expelled. The cold air drawn into the lung reaches the bronchial tubes, and as the vessels containing hot blood run alongside these tubes,

[1] " On some of the errors attributed to Aristotle."
[2] " History of Animals," i. 17.

the air cools it and carries off its superfluous heat. Some of the air which enters the lung gets from the bronchial tubes into the blood-vessels by transudation, for there is no direct communication between them; and this air, penetrating the body, rapidly cools the blood throughout the vessels. But Aristotle did not consider the "pneuma," which thus reached the interior of the blood-vessels, to be exactly the same thing as air—it was "a subtilized and condensed air."[1]   And this we now know to be oxygen.

The treatise "On the Generation of Animals" is an extraordinary production. "No ancient and few modern works equal it in comprehensiveness of detail and profound speculative insight. We here find some of the obscurest problems of biology treated with a mastery which, when we consider the condition of science at that day, is truly astounding. That there are many errors, many deficiencies, and not a little carelessness in the admission of facts, may be readily imagined; nevertheless at times the work is frequently on a level with, and occasionally even rises above, the speculations of many advanced embryologists."[2]

It commences with the statement that the present work is a sequel to that "On the Parts of Animals;" and first the masculine and feminine *principles* are defined. The masculine principle is the origin of all motion and

[1] See Professor Huxley's article already referred to.
[2] "Aristotle," by G. H. Lewes, p. 325.

generation; the feminine principle is the origin of the material generated. Aristotle's philosophy of nature was teleological, and the imperfect character of his anatomical knowledge often gives him occasion to explain particular phenomena by final causes. Thus animals producing soft-shelled eggs (*e.g.* cartilaginous fish and vipers) are said to do so because they have so little warmth that the external surface of the egg cannot be dried.

Among insects, some (*e.g.* grasshopper, cricket, ant, etc.) produce young in the ordinary way, by the union of the sexes; in other cases (*e.g.* flies and fleas) this union of the sexes results in the production of a *skolex;* while others have no parents, nor do they have congress—such are the ephemera, tipula, and the like. Aristotle dis-cusses and rejects the theory that the male reproductive element is derived from every part of the body. He concludes that "instead of saying that it comes *from* all parts of the body, we should say that it goes *to* them. It is not the nutrient fluid, but that which is *left over,* which is secreted. Hence the larger animals have fewer young than the smaller, for by them the consumption of nutrient material will be larger and the secretion less. Another point to be noticed is, that the nutrient fluid is universally distributed through the body, but each secretion has its separate organ. . . . It is thus intelligible why children resemble their parents, since that which makes all the parts of the body, resembles that which is left over as secretion : thus the hand, or the face, or the whole animal pre-exists in the sperm, though in an undifferentiated state (ἀδιορίστως) ; and what each of these is in actuality (ἐνεργείᾳ), such is the sperm in potentiality (δυνάμει)."

In later times the two great rival theories put forward to account for the development of the embryo have been—

(a) The theory of Evolution, which makes the embryo pre-existent in the germ, and only rendered visible by the unfolding and expansion of its organs.

(b) The theory of Epigenesis, which makes the embryo arise, by a series of successive differentiations, from a simple homogeneous mass into a complex heterogeneous organism.

The above quotation will show how closely Aristotle held to the theory of Epigenesis ; and in another place he says, " Not at once is the animal a man or a horse, for the end is last attained ; and the specific form is the end of each development."

Spontaneous generation is nowadays rejected by science ; but Aristotle went so far as to believe that insects, molluscs, and even eels, were spontaneously generated. It is, however, noteworthy, in view of modern investigations, that he looked upon *putrefying* matter as the source of such development.

A chapter of this work is devoted to the considera-
tion of the hereditary transmission of peculiarities from
parent to offspring.

The fifth and last book contains inquiries into the
cause of variation in the colour of the eyes and hair,
the abundance of hair, the sleep of the embryo, sight
and hearing, voice and the teeth.

Widely different opinions have been held from time
to time of the value of Aristotle's biological labours.
This philosopher's reputation has, perhaps, suffered most
from those who have praised him most. The praise
has often been of such an exaggerated character as to
have become unmeaning, and to have carried with it
the impression of insincerity on the part of the writer.
Such are the laudations of Cuvier. To say as he does,
" Alone, in fact, without predecessors, without having
borrowed anything from the centuries which had gone
before, since they had produced nothing enduring, the
disciple of Plato discovered and demonstrated more
truths and executed more scientific labours in a life of
sixty-two years than twenty centuries after him were
able to do," is of course to talk nonsense, for the method
which Aristotle applied was that which Hippocrates
had used so well before him ; and it is evident to any
one that both his predecessors and contemporaries are
frequently laid under contribution by Aristotle, although
the authority is rarely, if ever, stated by him unless he

is about to refute the view put forward. Exaggerated praise of any author has a tendency to excite depreciation correspondingly unjust and untrue. It has been so in the case of this great man. In the endeavour to depose him from the impossible position to which his panegyrists had exalted him, his detractors have gone to any length. The principal charges brought against his biological work have been inaccuracy and hasty generalization. In support of the charge of inaccuracy, some of the extraordinary statements which are met with in his works are adduced. "These," Professor Huxley says, " are not so much to be called errors as stupidities." Some, however, of the inaccuracies alleged against Aristotle are fancied rather than real. Thus he is charged with having represented that the arteries contained nothing but air ; that the aorta arose from the right ventricle ; that the heart did not beat in any other animal but man ; that reptiles had no blood, etc. ; although in reality he made no one of these assertions. There remain, nevertheless, the gross misstatements referred to above, and which really do occur. Such, for instance, as that there is but a single bone in the neck of the lion ; that there are more teeth in male than in female animals ; that the mouth of the dolphin is placed on the under surface of the body ; that the back of the skull is empty, etc. Although these absurdities undoubtedly occur in Aristotle's works, it by no means follows that he is responsible for them. Bearing in mind the curious history of the manuscripts of his treatises, we shall find it far more reasonable to conclude that such errors crept in during the process of correction and restoration, by men apparently ignorant of biology, than that (to take only one case) an observer who had distinguished the cetacea from fishes and had detected their hidden mammæ, discovered their lungs, and recognized the distinct character of their bones, should have been so blind as to fancy that the mouth of these animals was on the under surface of the body.

That Aristotle made hasty generalizations is true; but it was unavoidable. Biology was in so early a stage that a theory had often of necessity to be founded on a very slight basis of facts. Yet, notwithstanding this drawback, so great was the sagacity of this philosopher, that many of his generalizations, which he himself probably looked upon as temporary, have held their ground for twenty centuries, or, having been lost sight of, have been discovered and put forward as original by modern biologists. Thus "the advantage of physiological division of labour was first set forth," says Milne-Edwards, "by myself in 1827;" and yet Aristotle had said[1] that "whenever Nature is able to provide two separate instruments for two separate uses, without the one hampering the other, she does so, instead of acting

[1] " De Part. Anim.," iv. 6.

like a coppersmith, who for cheapness makes a spit-and-a-candlestick in one.[1] It is only when this is impossible that she uses one organ for several functions."

In conclusion, we may say that the great Stagirite expounded the true principles of science, and that when he failed his failure was caused by lack of materials. His desire for completeness, perhaps, tempted him at times to fill in gaps with such makeshifts as came to his hand; but no one knew better than he did that " theories must be abandoned unless their teachings tally with the indisputable results of observation."[2]

[1] ὀβελισκολύχνιον.
[2] " De Gener.," iii. 10, quoted by Dr. Ogle.

GALEN.

GALEN.

UNDER the Ptolemies a powerful stimulus was given to biological studies at Alexandria. Scientific knowledge was carried a step or two beyond the limit reached by Aristotle. Thus Erasistratus and Herophilus thoroughly investigated the structure and functions of the valves of the heart, and were the first to recognize the nerves as organs of sensation. But, unfortunately, no complete record of the interesting work carried on by these men has come down to our times. The first writer after Aristotle whose works arrest attention is Caius Plinius Secundus, whose so-called "Natural History," in thirty-seven volumes, remains to the present day as a monument of industrious compilation. But, as a biologist properly so called, Pliny is absolutely without rank, for he lacked that practical acquaintance with the subject which alone could enable him to speak with authority. Of information he had an almost inexhaustible store; of actual knowledge, the result of observation and experience, so far as biological studies were concerned, he had but little.   This was largely due to the encyclopædic character of the work he undertook; his mental powers were weighed down by an enormous mass of unarranged and ill-digested materials.   But it was due also to the peculiar bent of Pliny's mind.. He was not, like Aristotle, an original thinker; he was essentially a student of books, an immensely industrious but not always judicious compiler.   Often his selections from other works prove that he failed to appreciate the relative importance of the different subjects to which he made reference.   His knowledge of the Greek language appears, too, to have been defective, for he gives at times the wrong Latin names to objects described by his Greek authorities. To these defects must be added his marvellous readiness to believe any statement, provided only that it was uncommon; while, on the other hand, he showed an indefensible scepticism in regard to what was really deserving of attention.   The chief value of his work consists in the historical and chronological notes of the progress of some of the subjects of which he treats— fragments of writings which would otherwise be lost to us.   Pliny was killed in the destruction of Pompeii, A.D. 79.

Claudius Galenus was born at Pergamus, in Asia Minor, in the hundred and thirty-first year of the Christian era. Few writers ever exercised for so long a time such an undisputed sway over the opinions of mankind as did this wonderful man. His authority was estimated at a much higher rate than that of all the biological writers combined who flourished during a period of more than twelve centuries, and it was often considered a sufficient argument against a hypothesis, or even an alleged matter of fact, that it was contrary to Galen.

Endowed by nature with a penetrating genius and a mind of restless energy, he was eminently qualified to profit by a comprehensive and liberal education. And such he received. His father, Nicon, an architect, was a man of learning and ability—a distinguished mathematician and an astronomer—and seems to have devoted much time and care to the education of his son. The youth appears to have studied philosophy successively in the schools of the Stoics, Academics, Peripatetics, and Epicureans, without attaching himself exclusively to any one of these, and to have taken from each what he thought to be the most essential parts of their system, rejecting, however, altogether the tenets of the Epicureans. At the age of twenty-one, on the death of his father, he went to Smyrna to continue the study of medicine, to which he had now devoted himself. After leaving this place and having travelled extensively, he took up his residence at Alexandria, which was then the most favourable spot for the pursuit of medical studies. Here he is said to have remained until he was twenty-eight years of age, when his reputation secured

E

his appointment, in his native city of Pergamus, to the
office of physician in charge of the athletes in the
gymnasia situated within the precincts of the temple of
Æsculapius.   For five or six years he lived in Pergamus,
and then a revolt compelled him to leave his native
town.   The advantages offered by Rome led him to
remove thither and take up his residence in the capital
of the world.   Here his skill, sagacity, and knowledge
soon brought him into notice, and excited the jealousy
of the Roman doctors, which was still further increased
by some wonderful cures the young Greek physician
succeeded in effecting.   Possibly it was owing to the
ill feeling shown to Galen that, on the outbreak of
an epidemic a year afterwards, he left the imperial city
and proceeded to Brindisi, and embarked for Greece.
It was his intention to devote his time to the study
of natural history, and for this purpose he visited
Cyprus, Palestine, and Lemnos.   While at the last-named
place, however, he was suddenly summoned to Aquileia
to meet the Emperors Marcus Aurelius and Lucius
Verus.   He travelled through Thrace and Macedonia on
foot, met the imperial personages, and prepared for them
a medicine, for which he seems to have been famous,
and which is spoken of as the *theriac.*   It was probably
some combination of opium with various aromatics and
stimulants, for antidotes of many different kinds were
habitually taken by the Romans to preserve them from

the ill effects of poison and of the bites of venomous animals.[1]

With the Emperor M. Aurelius he returned to Rome, and became afterwards doctor to the young Emperor Commodus. He did not, however, remain for a long period at Rome, and probably passed the greater part of the rest of his life in his native country.

Although the date of his death is not positively known, yet it appears from a passage[2] in his writings that he was living in the reign of Septimius Severus; and Suidas seems to have reason for asserting that he reached his seventieth year.

Galen's writings represent the common depository of the anatomical knowledge of the day; what he had learnt from many teachers, rather than the results of his own personal research. Roughly speaking, they deal with the following subjects: Anatomy and Physiology, Dietetics and Hygiene, Pathology, Diagnosis and Semeiology, Pharmacy and Materia Medica, Therapeutics.

The only works of this voluminous writer at which we can here glance are those dealing with Anatomy and Physiology. These exhibit numerous illustrations of Galen's familiarity with practical anatomy, although it was most likely comparative rather than human

---

[1] Hence the name θηρίακαι.
[2] "De Antidotis," i. 13, vol. xiv. p. 65, Kuhn.

anatomy at which he especially worked.   Indeed, he seems to have had but few opportunities of carrying on human dissections, for he thinks himself happy in having been able to examine at Alexandria two human skeletons ; and he recommends the dissection of monkeys because of their exact resemblance to man.   To this disadvantage may, perhaps, be attributed the readiness, which sometimes appears, to assume identity of organization between man and the brutes.   Thus, because in certain animals he found a double biliary duct, he concluded the same to be the case in man, and in one instance he proceeded to deduce the cause of disease from this erroneous assumption.

He supposed that there were three modes of existence in man, namely—

(*a*) The nutritive, which was common to all animals and plants, of which the liver was the source.

(*b*) The vital, of which the heart was the source.

(*c*) The rational, of which the brain was the source.

Again, he considered that the animal economy possessed four natural powers—

(1) The attractive.

(2) The alterative or assimilative.

(3) The retentive or digestive.

(4) The expulsive.

Like his predecessors, he asserted that there were four humours, namely, blood, yellow bile, black bile, and aqueous serum. He held that it was the office of the liver to complete the process of sanguification commenced in the stomach, and that during this process the yellow bile was attracted by the branches of the hepatic duct and gall-bladder; the black bile being attracted by the spleen, and the aqueous humour by the two kidneys; while the liver itself retained the pure blood, which was afterwards attracted by the heart through the vena cava, by whose ramifications it was distributed to the various parts of the body.

Following Aristotle especially, he regarded hair, nails, arteries, veins, cartilage, bone, ligament, membranes, glands, fat, and muscle as the simplest constituents of the body, formed immediately from the blood, and perfectly homogeneous in character. The organic members, *e.g.* lungs, liver, etc., he looked upon as formed of several of the foregoing simple parts.

The osteology contained in Galen's works is nearly as perfect as that of the present day. He correctly names and describes the bones and sutures of the cranium; notices the quadrilateral shape of the parietals, the peculiar situation and shape of the sphenoid, and the form and character of the ethmoid, malar, maxillary, and nasal bones. He divides the vertebral columns into cervical, dorsal, and lumbar portions.

With regard to the nervous system, he taught that the nerves of the senses are distinct from those which impart the power of motion to muscles—that the former are derived from the anterior parts of the brain, while the latter arise from the posterior portion, or from the spinal cord. He maintained that the nerves of the finer senses are formed of matter too soft to be the vehicles of muscular motion; whereas, on the other hand, the nerves of motion are too hard to be susceptible of fine sensibility. His description of the method of demonstrating the different parts of the brain by dissection is very interesting, and, like his references to various instruments and contrivances, proves him to have been a practical and experienced anatomist.

In his description of the organs and process of nutrition, absorption by the veins of the stomach is correctly noticed, and the union of the mesenteric veins into one common *vena portæ* is pointed out. The communications between the ramifications of the vena portæ and of the proper veins of the liver are supposed by Galen to be effected by means of anastomosing pores or channels. Although it is evident that Galen was ignorant of the true absorbent system, yet he appears to have been aware of the *lacteals;* for he says that in addition to those mesenteric veins which by their union form the vena portæ, there are visible in every part of the mesentery other veins, proceeding also from the intestines, which terminate in glands; and he supposes that these veins are intended for the nourishment of the intestines themselves. Some of Galen's contemporaries asserted that upon exposing the mesentery of a sucking animal several small vessels were seen filled *first* with air, and *afterwards* with milk. They had, doubtless, mistaken colourless lymph for air; but Galen ridicules both assertions, and thereby shows that he had not examined the contents of the lacteals. This is somewhat remarkable, because as a rule he omitted no opportunity of determining with certainty, by vivisection and experiments on living animals, the uses of the various parts of the body. As an illustration of this, we have his correct statement, established by experiment, that the pylorus acts as a valve *only* during the process of digestion, and that it is relaxed when digestion is completed.

He recognizes that the flesh of the heart is somewhat different to that of the muscles of voluntary motion. Its fibres are described as being arranged in longitudinal and transverse bundles; the former by their contractions shortening the organ, the latter compressing and narrowing it. Such statements show that he regarded the heart as essentially muscular. He thought, however, that it was entirely destitute of nerves. Although he admitted that possibly it had one small branch derived from the *nervus vagus* sent to it, yet he entirely overlooked the great nervous plexus surrounding the roots of the blood-vessels, from which branches proceed in company with the branches of the coronary arteries and veins, and penetrate the muscular substance of the ventricles. He endeavoured to prove, by experiment, observation, and reasoning, that the arteries as well as the veins contained blood, and in this connection he tells an amusing story. A certain teacher of anatomy, who had declared that the aorta contained no blood, was earnestly desired by his pupils, who were ardent disciples of Galen, to exhibit the requisite demonstration, they themselves offering animals for the experiment. He, however, after various subterfuges, declined, until they promised to give him a suitable remuneration, which they raised by subscription among themselves to the amount of a thousand drachmæ (perhaps £30). The professor, being thus compelled to commence the experiment, totally failed in his attempt to cut down upon the aorta, to the no small amusement of his pupils, who, thereupon taking up the experiment themselves, made an opening into the thorax in the way in which they had been instructed by Galen, passed one ligature round the aorta at the part where it attaches itself to the spine, and another at its origin, and then, by opening the intervening portion of the artery, showed that blood was contained in it.

The arteries, Galen thought, possessed a pulsative and · attractive power of their own, independently of the heart, the moment of their dilatation being the moment of their activity. They, in fact, *drew* their charge from the heart, as the heart by its diastole *drew* its charge from the vena cava and the pulmonary vein. The pulse of the arteries, he also thought, was propagated by their coats, not by the wave of blood thrown into them by the heart. He taught that at every systole of the arteries a certain portion of their contents was discharged at their extremities, namely, by the exhalents and secretory vessels. Though he demonstrated the anastomosis of arteries and veins, he nowhere hints his belief that the contents of the former pass into the latter, to be conveyed back to the heart, and from it to be again diffused over the body. He made a near approach to the Harveian theory of the circulation, as Harvey himself admits in his " De Motu Cordis;"[1] but the grand point of difference between Galen and Harvey is the question whether or not, at every systole of the left ventricle, more blood is thrown out than is expended on exhalation, secretion, and nutrition. Upon this point Galen held the negative, and Harvey, as we all know, the affirmative.

The famous Asclepiads held that respiration was for the generation of the soul itself, breath and life being thus considered to be identical. Hippocrates thought it was for the nutrition and refrigeration of the innate

---

[1] "Ex ipsius etiam Galeni verbis hanc veritatem confirmari posse, scilicet : non solum posse sanguinem e vena arteriosa in arteriam venosam et inde in sinistrum ventriculum cordis, et postea in arterias transmitti."—" De Motu Cordis," cap. vii.

heat, Aristotle for its ventilation, Erasistratus for the filling of the arteries with spirits. All these opinions are discussed and commented upon by Galen, who determines the purposes of respiration to be (1) to preserve the animal heat; (2) to evacuate from the blood the products of combustion.

He conjectured that there was in atmospheric air not only a quality friendly to the vital spirit, but also a quality inimical to it, which conjecture he drew from observation of the various phenomena accompanying the support and the extinction of flame; and he says that if we could find out why flame is extinguished by absence of the air, we might then know the nature of that substance which imparts warmth to the blood during the process of respiration.

On another occasion he says that it is evidently the *quality* and not the *quantity* of the air which is necessary to life. He further shows that he recognized the analogy between respiration and combustion, by comparing the lungs to a lamp, the heart to its wick, the blood to the oil, and the animal heat to the flame.

From certain observations in various parts of his works, it appears that, although ignorant of the doctrine of atmospheric pressure, he was acquainted with some of its practical effects. Thus, he says, if you put one end of an open tube under water and suck out the air with the other end, you will draw up water into the mouth, and that it is in this way that infants extract the milk from the mother's breast.

Again, Erasistratus supposed that the vapour of charcoal and of certain pits and wells was fatal to life because *lighter* than common air, but Galen maintained it to be *heavier.*

He describes two kinds of respiration, one by the mouths of the arteries of the lungs, and one by the mouths of the arteries of the skin. In each case, he says, the surrounding air is drawn into the vessels during their diastole, for the purpose of cooling the blood, and during their systole the fuliginous particles derived from the blood and other fluids of the body are forced out.

He considers the diaphragm to be the principal muscle of respiration, but he makes a clear distinction between ordinary respiration, which he calls a natural and involuntary effort, and that deliberate and forced respiration which is obedient to the will; and he says that there are different muscles for the two purposes. Elsewhere he particularly points out the two sets of intercostal muscles and their mode of action, of which, before his time, he asserts that anatomists were ignorant.

He describes various effects produced on respiration and on the voice by the division of those nerves which are connected with the thorax; and shows particularly the effect of dividing the recurrent branch of his sixth pair of cerebral nerves (the pneumogastric of modern anatomy). He explains how it happens that after division of the spinal cord, provided that division be *beneath* the lower termination of the neck, the diaphragm will still continue to act—in consequence, namely, of the origin of the phrenic nerve being *above* the lower termination of the neck.

Before the time of Galen the medical profession was divided into several sects, *e.g.* Dogmatici, Empirici, Eclectici, Pneumatici, and Episynthetici, who were always disputing with one another. After his time all sects seem to have merged in his followers. The subsequent Greek and Roman biological writers were mere compilers from his works, and as soon as his writings were translated into Arabic they were at once adopted throughout the East to the exclusion of all others. He remained paramount throughout the civilized world until within the last three hundred years. In the records of the College of Physicians of England we read that Dr. Geynes was cited before the college in 1559 for impugning the infallibility of Galen, and was only admitted again into the privileges of his fellowship on acknowledgment of his error, and humble recantation signed with his own hand. Kurt Sprengel has well said that "if the physicians who remained so faithfully attached to Galen's system had inherited his penetrating mind, his observing glance, and his depth, the art of healing would have approached the limit of perfection before all the other sciences; but it was written in the book of destiny that mind and reason were to bend under the yoke of superstition and barbarism, and were only to emerge after centuries of lethargic sleep."

VESALIUS.

VESALIUS.

THE authority of Galen, at once a despotism and a religion, was scarcely ever called in question until the sixteenth century. No attempt worth recording was made during thirteen hundred years to extend the boundary of scientific knowledge in anatomy and physiology. It is true that the scholastic philosopher, Albertus Magnus, who was for a short time (1260–1262) Bishop of Ratisbon, in the middle of the thirteenth century wrote a " History of Animals," which was a remarkable production for the age in which he lived; although Sir Thomas Browne, in his famous " Enquiries into Common Errors," speaks of these " Tractates " as requiring to be received with caution, adding as regards Albertus that "he was a man who much advanced these opinions by the authoritie of his name, and delivered most conceits, with strickt enquirie into few."

As regards human anatomy, it was considered, during the Middle Ages, to be impiety to touch with a scalpel "the dead image of God," as man's body was called.

F

Mundinus, the professor of medicine at Bologna from 1315 to 1318, was the first to attempt any such thing. He exhibited the public dissection of three bodies, but by this created so great a scandal that he gave up the practice, and contented himself with publishing a work, " De Anatome," which formed a sort of commentary on Galen. This work, with additions, continued to be the text-book of the schools until the time of Vesalius, who founded the study of anatomy as nowadays pursued.

Andreas Vesalius was born at Brussels, on the last day of the year 1514, of a family which for several generations had been eminent for medical attainments. He was sent as a boy to Louvain, where he spent the greater part of his leisure in researches into the mechanism of the lower animals. He was a born dissector, who, after careful examination, in his early days, of rats, moles, dogs, cats, monkeys, and the like, came, in after-life, to be dissatisfied with any less knowledge of the anatomy of man.

He acquired great proficiency in the scholarship of the day. Indeed the Latin, in which he afterwards wrote his great work, is so singularly pure that one of his detractors pretended that Vesalius must have got some good scholar to write the Latin for him. Latin was not the only language in which he was proficient; he added Greek and Arabic to his other accomplishments, and this for the purpose of reading the great biological works in the languages in which they were originally written. From

Louvain the youth went to Paris, where he studied anatomy under a most distinguished physician, Sylvius. It was the practice of that illustrious professor to read to his class Galen on the " Use of Parts," omitting nearly all the sections where exact knowledge of anatomical detail was necessary. Sometimes an attempt was made to illustrate the lecture by the dissection of a dog, but such illustration more often exposed the professor's ignorance than it added to the student's knowledge. Indirectly, however, it did good, for whenever Sylvius, after having tried in vain to demonstrate some muscle, or nerve, or vein, left the room, his pupil Vesalius slipped down to the table, dissected out the part with great neatness, and triumphantly called the professor's attention to it on his return.

Besides studying under Sylvius, Vesalius had for his teacher at Paris the famous Winter, of Andernach, who was physician to Francis I. This learned man, in a work published three years after this period, speaks of Vesalius as a youth of great promise. At the age of nineteen Vesalius returned to Louvain ; and here for the first time he openly demonstrated from the human subject. In this connection a somewhat ghastly story is told, which serves to show the intensity of the enthusiasm with which our anatomist was inspired. On a certain evening it chanced that Vesalius, in company with a friend, had rambled out of the gates of Louvain to a spot where the bodies of executed criminals were wont to be exposed. A noted robber had been executed. His body had been chained to a stake and slowly roasted; and the birds had so entirely stripped the bones of every vestige of flesh, that a perfect skeleton, complete and clean, was suspended before the eyes of the anatomist, who had been striving hitherto to piece together such a thing out of the bones of many people, gathered as occasion offered. Mounting upon the shoulder of his friend, Vesalius ascended the charred stake and forcibly tore away the limbs, leaving only the trunk, which was securely bound by iron chains. With these stolen bones under their clothes the two youths returned to Louvain. In the night, however, and alone, the sturdy Vesalius found his way again to the place—which to most men, at any rate in those times, would have been associated with unspeakable horrors—and there, by sheer force, wrenched away the trunk, and buried it. Then leisurely and carefully, day after day, he smuggled through the city gates bone after bone. Afterwards, when he had set up the perfect skeleton in his own house, he did not hesitate to demonstrate from it. But such an act of daring plunder could not escape detection, and he was banished from Louvain for the offence. This story is here quoted only to show the extraordinary physical and moral courage which the anatomist possessed; which upheld him through toils, dangers, and disgusts; and by which he was strengthened to carry on, even in a cruel and superstitious age, and placed, as he was, on the very threshold of the Inquisition, a work at all times repulsive to flesh and blood.

After serving for a short time as a surgeon in the army of the Emperor Charles V., Vesalius went to Italy, where he at once attracted the attention of the most learned men, and became, at the age of twenty-two, Professor of Anatomy at the University of Padua. This was the first purely anatomical professorship that had been established out of the funds of any university. For seven years he held the office, and he was at the same time professor at Bologna and at Pisa. During these years his lectures were always well attended, for they were a striking innovation on the tameness of conventional routine. In each university the services of the professor were confined to a short course of demonstrations, so that his duties were complete when he had spent, during the winter, a few weeks at each of the three towns in succession. He then returned to Venice, which he appears to have made his head-quarters. At this city, as well as at Pisa, special facilities were offered to the professor for obtaining bodies either of condemned criminals or others. At Padua and Bologna the enthusiasm of the students, who became resurrectionists on their teacher's behalf, kept the lecture-table supplied with specimens. They were in the habit of watching all

the symptoms in men dying of a fatal malady, and noting
where, after death, such men were buried. The seclusion
of the graveyard was then invaded, and the corpse
secretly conveyed by Andreas to his chamber, and con-
cealed sometimes in his own bed. A diligent search was
at once made to determine accurately the cause of death.
This pitiless zeal for correct details in anatomy, associated
as it was with indefatigable practice in physic, appeared
to Vesalius, as it does to his successors of to-day, to be
the only satisfactory method of acquiring that knowledge
which is essential to a doctor.   Thus it was that he, who
at the age of twenty-two was able to name, with his eyes
blindfolded, any human bone put into his hand, who
was deeply versed in comparative anatomy, and had
more accurate knowledge of the human frame than any
graybeard of the time, enjoyed afterwards a reputation
as a physician which was unbounded.   One illustration
of his sagacity in diagnosis will suffice. A patient of
two famous court physicians at Madrid had a big and
wonderful tumour on the loins. It would have been
easily recognized in these days as an aneurismal tumour,
but it greatly puzzled the two doctors. Vesalius was
therefore consulted, and said, " There is a blood-vessel
dilated ; that tumour is full of blood." They were sur-
prised at such a strange opinion ; but the man died, the
tumour was opened ; blood was actually found in it, and
we are told *in admirationem rapti fuère omnes.*

It was not until after Vesalius had been three years professor that he began to distrust the infallibility of Galen's anatomical teaching. Constant practical experience in dissection, both human and comparative, slowly convinced him that—great anatomist as the "divus homo" had undoubtedly been—his statements were not only incomplete, but often wrong; further, that Galen very rarely wrote from actual inspection of the human subject, but based his teaching on a belief that the structure of a monkey was exactly similar to that of a man. With this conviction established, Vesalius proceeded to note with great care all the discrepancies between the text of Galen and the actual parts which it endeavoured to describe, and in this way a volume of considerable thickness was soon formed, consisting entirely of annotations upon Galen. The generally received authorities being thus found to be unreliable, it became necessary in the next place to collect and arrange the fundamental facts of anatomy upon a new and sounder basis. To this task Vesalius, at the age of twenty-five, devoted himself, and began his famous work on the "Fabric of the Human Body." Owing possibly to the good fortune of his family, and to the income which he derived from his professorships, Andreas was able to secure for his work the aid of some of the best artists of the day. To Jean Calcar, one of the ablest of the pupils of Titian, are due the splendid anatomical plates which illustrate the " Corporis Humani Fabrica," and which are incomparably better than those of any work which preceded it. To him most likely is due also the woodcut which adorns the first page, and which represents the young Vesalius, wearing professor's robes, standing at a lecture-table and pointing out, from a robust subject that lies before him, the inner secrets of the human body; while the tiers of benches that surround the professor are completely crowded with grave doctors struggling to see, even climbing upon the railings to do so.

But throughout the work the plates are used simply to illustrate and elucidate the text, and the information furnished in the latter is minute and accurate, and stated in well-polished Latin. As the author proceeds, he finds it necessary to disagree with Galen, and the reasons for this disagreement are given. The inevitable result follows that Vesalius is placed at issue not only with " the divine man," but also with all those who for thirteen centuries had unquestioningly followed him. Such a result Vesalius must have foreseen. It was not, therefore, a great surprise to him, perhaps, to receive, soon after the publication of his work, a violent onslaught from his old master Sylvius. He simply replied to it by a letter full of respect and friendly feeling, inquiring wherein he had been guilty of error. The answer he got was that he must show proper respect for Galen, if he wished to be regaided as a friend of Sylvius.

In 1546, three years after the publication of his great work, Andreas was summoned to Ratisbon to exercise his skill upon the emperor, and from that date he was ranked among the court physicians. In the same year, 1546, in a long letter, entitled " De usu Radicis Chinæ," he not only treats of the medicine by which the emperor's health had been restored, but he vindicates his teaching against his assailants, and again gives cumulative proof of the fact that Galen had dissected only brutes.

It was the practice of Vesalius, while he was professor in Italy, to issue a public notice the day before each demonstration, stating the time at which it would take place, and inviting all who decried his errors to attend and make their own dissections from his subject, and confound him openly. It does not appear that any one was rash enough ever to accept the challenge; yet, although the majority of the young men were on the side of Vesalius, the older teachers continued to regard him as a heretic, and in 1551 Sylvius published a bitterly personal attack. It was nothing to him that the results of actual dissection were against him—he even went so far as to assert that the men of his time were constructed somewhat differently to those of the time of Galen ! Thus, to the proof that Vesalius gave that the carpal bones were not absolutely without marrow, as Galen had asserted, Sylvius replied that the bones were harder and more solid among the ancients, and were, in consequence, destitute of medullary substance. Again, when Vesalius showed that Galen was wrong in describing the human femur and humerus as greatly curved, Sylvius explained the discrepancy by saying that the wearing of narrow garments by the moderns had straightened the limbs.

Through these attacks, however, the writings of Vesalius fell into somewhat bad odour in the court; for in that very superstitious age there was a kind of vague dread felt of reading the works of a man against whom such serious charges of arrogance and impiety were brought. And so it came about that when he received the summons to take up his residence permanently at Madrid, and the orthodoxy of the day seemed for the moment to triumph, in a fit of proud indignation, he burned all his manuscripts; destroying a huge volume of annotations upon Galen; a whole book of medical formulæ; many original notes on drugs; the copy of Galen from which he lectured, and which was covered with marginal notes of new observations that had occurred to him while demonstrating; and the paraphrases of the books of Rhases, in which the knowledge of the Arabian was collated with that of the Greeks and others. The produce of the labour of many years was thus reduced to ashes in a short fit of passion, and from this time Vesalius lived no more for controversy or study. He gave himself up to pleasure and the pursuit of wealth, resting on his reputation and degenerating into a mere courtier. As a practitioner he was held in high esteem. When the life of Don Carlos, Philip's son, was despaired of, it was Vesalius who was called in, and who, seeing that the surgeons had bound up the wound in the head so tightly that an abscess had formed, promptly brought relief to the patient by cutting into the pericranium. The cure of the prince, however, was attributed by the court to the intercession of St. Diego, and it is possible that on the subject of this alleged miraculous recovery Vesalius may have expressed his opinion rather more strongly than it was safe for a Netherlander to do. At any rate, the priests always looked upon him with dislike and suspicion, and at length they and the other enemies of the great anatomist had their revenge.

A young Spanish nobleman had died, and Vesalius, who had attended him, obtained permission to ascertain, if possible, by a post-mortem examination, the cause of death. On opening the body, the heart was said—by the bystanders—to beat; and a charge, not merely of murder, but of impiety also, was brought against Vesalius. It was hoped by his persecutors that the latter charge would be brought before the Inquisition, and result in more rigorous punishment than any that would be inflicted by the judges of the common law. The King of Spain, however, interfered and saved him, on condition that he should make a pilgrimage to the Holy Land. Accordingly he set out from Madrid for Venice, and

thence to Cyprus, from which place he went on to
Jerusalem, and was returning, not to Madrid, but to
Padua, where the professorship of physic had been
offered him, when he suffered shipwreck on the island
of Zante, and there perished miserably of hunger and
grief, on October 15, 1564, before he had reached the
age of fifty. His body was found by a travelling gold-
smith, who recognized, notwithstanding their starved
outlines, the features of the renowned anatomist, and
respectfully buried his remains and raised a statue to his
memory.

Two of the works of this great man have been already
referred to, namely: "De corporis Humani Fabrica;"
"De usu Radicis Chinæ." Besides these the following
have appeared : " Examen Observationum Gabrielis
Fallopii ; " " Gabrielis Cunei Examen, Apologiæ Fran-
cisci Putei pro Galeno in Anatome ; " a great work on
Surgery in seven books.

With respect to the last of these, it may be sufficient
to remark that there is every reason to believe that the
name of the famous anatomist was stolen after his death
to give value to the production, which was compiled and
published by a Venetian named Bogarucci; and that
Vesalius is not responsible for the contents.

The other works are undoubtedly genuine. In 1562
Andreas seems to have been roused for a short time
from the lethargy into which he had sunk, by an attack

from Franciscus Puteus; for to this attack a reply appeared—from a writer calling himself Gabriel Cuneus—which has always been attributed by the most competent authorities to Vesalius himself. In this rather long work, covering as it does more than fifty pages in the folio edition, the views of Vesalius, which are at variance with Galen, are gone through *seriatim* and defended.

In 1561 Fallopius, who had studied under Vesalius, published his "Anatomical Observations," containing several points in which he had extended the knowledge of anatomy beyond the limits reached by his master. He had taught publicly for thirteen years at Ferrara, and had presided for eight years over an anatomical school, so that he was no novice in the field of biology. Yet so completely had Vesalius lost the philosophic temperament that he regarded this publication as an infringement of his rights, and in this spirit wrote an " Examen Observationum Fallopii," in which he decried the friend who had made improvements on himself, as he had been decried for his improvements on Galen. The manuscript of this work, finished at the end of December, 1561, was committed by the author to the care of Paulus Teupulus of Venice, orator to the King of Spain, who was to give it to Fallopius. The orator, however, did not reach Padua until after the death of Fallopius, and he consequently retained the document until Vesalius, on his way to Jerusalem, took possession of it, and caused it to be published without delay.   It appeared at Venice in 1564.[1]

The letter on the China root—a plant we know nowadays as sarsaparilla—by the use of which the emperor's recovery was effected, has been already referred to.   It was addressed to the anatomist's friend, Joachim Roelants. Very little space, however, is taken up with a description of the medicine which gives title to the letter.   Something certainly is said of the history and nature of the plant, the preparation of the decoction and its effects ; but the writer soon introduces the subject which was at that time of very vital importance to him, namely, his position with regard to the statements of Galen and his followers.   He collects together various assertions of the Greek anatomist, on the bones, the muscles and ligaments, the relations of veins and arteries, the nerves, the character of the peritoneum, the organs of the thorax, the skull and its contents, etc., and shows from each and all of these that reference had not been made to the human subject, and that therefore the statements were unreliable.

To the work on the " Fabric of the Human Body " we have already alluded, as well as to the causes which led to its being written.   More than half of this great treatise

---

[1] See Professor Morley's article on " Anatomy in Long Clothes," in *Fraser's Magazine*, 1853, from which most of the facts in this sketch have been taken.

is occupied with a minute description of the build of the human body—its bones, cartilages, ligaments, and muscles. It may have been owing to the thorough acquaintance which Vesalius showed with these parts that his detractors pretended afterwards that he only understood superficial injuries. But other branches of anatomy are fully dealt with. The veins and arteries are described in the third book, and the nerves in the fourth ; the organs of nutrition and reproduction are treated of in the next; while the remaining two books are devoted to descriptions of the heart and brain.

Vesalius gives a good account of the sphenoid bone, with its large and small wings and its pterygoid processes ; and he accurately describes the vestibule in the interior of the temporal bone. He shows the sternum to consist, in the adult, of three parts and the sacrum of five or six. He discovered the valve which guards the *foramen ovale* in the fœtus ; and he not only verified the observation of Etienne as to the valve-like fold guarding the entrance of each hepatic vein into the inferior vena cava, but he also fully described the *vena azygos*. He observed, too, the canal which passes in the fœtus between the umbilical vein and vena cava, and which has since been known as the *ductus venosus*. He was the first to study and describe the mediastinum, correcting the error of the ancients, who believed that this duplicature of the pleura contained a portion of the lungs. He described the omentum and its connections with the stomach, the spleen, and the colon ; and he enunciated the first correct views of the structure of the pylorus, noticing at the same time the small size of the cæcal appendix in man. His account of the anatomy of the brain is fuller than that of any of his predecessors, but he does not appear to have well understood the inferior recesses, and his description of the nerves is confused by regarding the optic as the first pair, the third as the fifth, and the fifth as the seventh. The ancients believed the optic nerve to be hollow for the conveyance of the visual spirit, but Vesalius showed that no such tube existed. He observed the elevation and depression of the brain during respiration, but being ignorant of the circulation of the blood, he wrongly explained the phenomenon.

Exclusively an anatomist, he makes but brief references in his great work to the functions of the organs which he describes. Where he differs from Galen on these matters he does so apologetically. He follows him in regarding the heart as the seat of the emotions and passions—the hottest of all the viscera and source of heat of the whole body ; although he does not, as Aristotle did, look upon the heart as giving rise to the nerves. He considers the heart to be in ceaseless motion, alternately dilating and contracting, but the diastole is in his opinion the influential act of the organ. He knows that eminences or projections are present in the veins, and indeed speaks of them as being analogous to the valves of the heart, but he denies to them the office of valves. To him the motion of the blood was of a to-and-fro kind, and valves in the veins acting as such would have interfered with anything of the sort. He expresses clearly the idea, that was entertained in the old physiology, of the attractions exerted by the various parts of the body for the blood; and especially that of the veins and heart for the blood itself. "The right sinus of the heart," he says, "attracts blood from the vena cava, and the left attracts air from the lungs through the *arteria venalis* (pulmonary vein), the blood itself being attracted by the veins in general, the vital spirit by the arteries." Again, he speaks of the blood filtering through the septum between the ventricles as if through a sieve, although he knows perfectly well from his dissection that the septum is quite impervious.

It will thus be seen that the physiological teaching of Galen was left undisturbed by Vesalius.

HARVEY.

HARVEY.

The importance of Harvey's discovery of the circulation of the blood can only be properly estimated by bearing in mind what was done by his predecessors in the same field of inquiry. Aristotle had taught that in man and in the higher brutes the blood was elaborated from the food in the liver, conveyed to the heart, and thence distributed by it through the veins to the whole body. Erasistratus and Herophilus held that, while the veins carried blood from the heart to the members, the arteries carried a subtle kind of air or spirit. Galen discovered that the arteries were not merely air-pipes, but that they contained blood as well as vital air or spirit. Sylvius, the teacher of Vesalius, was aware of the presence of valves in the veins ; and Fabricius, Harvey's teacher at Padua, described them much more accurately than Sylvius had done ; but neither of these men had a true idea of the significance of the structures of which they wrote. Servetus, the friend and contemporary of Vesalius, writing in 1533, correctly described the course of the

lesser circulation in the following words : "This communication (*i.e.* between the right and left sides of the
heart) does not take place through the partition of the
heart, as is generally believed; but by another admirable
contrivance, whereby from the right ventricle the subtle
blood is agitated in a lengthened course through the
lungs, wherein prepared, it becomes of a crimson colour,
and from the vena arterialis (pulmonary artery) is transferred into the arteria venalis (pulmonary vein). Mingled
with the inspired air in the arteria venalis, freed by respiration from fuliginous matter, and become a suitable
home of the vital spirit, it is attracted at length into the
left ventricle of the heart by the diastole of the organ."
But when Servetus comes to speak of the systemic circulation, what he has to say is as old as Galen.

The opinions, therefore, on the subject of the blood
and its distribution which were prevalent at the end of
the sixteenth century prove—

(1) That although the blood was not regarded as
stagnant, yet its circulation, such as is nowadays recognized, was unknown ;

(2) That one kind of blood was thought to flow from
the liver to the right ventricle, and thence to
the lungs and general system by the veins, while
another kind flowed from the left ventricle to
the lungs and general system by the arteries ;

(3) That the septum of the heart was regarded as

admitting of the passage of blood directly from the right to the left side ;

(4) That there was no conception of the functions of the heart as the motor power of the movement of the blood, for biologists of that day doubted whether the substance of the heart were really muscular; they supposed the pulsations to be due to expansion of the spirits it contained ; they believed the only dynamic effect which it had on the blood to be that of sucking it in during its active diastole, and they supposed the chief use of its constant movements to be the due mixture of blood and spirits.

This was the state of knowledge before Harvey's time. By his great work he established—

(1) That the blood flows continuously in a circuit through the whole body, the force propelling it in this unwearied round being the rhythmical contractions of the muscular walls of the heart ;

(2) That a portion only of the blood is expended in nutrition each time that it circulates ;

(3) That the blood conveyed in the systemic arteries communicates heat as well as nourishment throughout the body, instead of exerting a cooling influence, as was vulgarly supposed ; and

(4) That the pulse is not produced by the arteries enlarging and so filling, but by the arteries being filled with blood and so enlarging.

We can now consider the method by which Harvey arrived at these results. The work, "De Motu Cordis et Sanguinis," after giving an account of the views of preceding physiologists, ancient and modern, commences with a description of the heart as seen in a living animal when the chest has been laid open and the pericardium removed. Three circumstances are noted—

(*a*) The heart becomes erect, strikes the chest, and gives a beat;

(*b*) It is constricted in every direction;

(*c*) Grasped by the hand, it is felt to become harder during the contraction.

From these circumstances it is inferred—

(1) That the action of the heart is essentially of the same nature as that of voluntary muscles, which become hard and condensed when they act;

(2) That, as the effect of this, the capacity of the cavities is diminished, and the blood is expelled;

(3) That the intrinsic motion of the heart is the systole, and not the diastole, as previously imagined.

The motions of the arteries are next shown to be dependent upon the action of the heart, because the arteries are distended by the wave of blood that is thrown into them, being filled like sacs or bladders, and not expanding like bellows. These conclusions are confirmed by the jerking way in which blood flows from a cut artery.

In the heart itself two distinct motions are observed—first of the auricles, and then of the ventricles. These alternate contractions and dilatations can have but one result, namely, to force the blood from the auricle to the ventricle, and from the ventricle, on the right side, by the pulmonary artery to the lungs, and on the left side by the aorta to the system.

These considerations suggest to the mind of Harvey the idea of the circulation. " I began to think," he says, "whether there might not be a motion, as it were, in a circle." This is next established by proving the three following propositions :—

(1) The blood is incessantly transmitted by the action of the heart from the vena cava to the arteries in such quantity that it cannot be supplied from the ingesta, and in such wise that the whole mass must very quickly pass through the organ ;

(2) The blood, under the influence of the arterial pulse, enters, and is impelled in a continuous, equable, and incessant stream through every part and member of the body, in much larger quantity than were sufficient for nutrition, or than the whole mass of fluids could supply ;

(3) The veins in like manner return this blood incessantly to the heart from all parts and members
of the body.

As to the first proposition Harvey says, " Did the
heart eject but two drachms of blood on each contraction,
and the beats in half an hour were a thousand, the
quantity expelled in that time would amount to twenty
pounds and ten ounces; and were the quantity an ounce,
it would be as much as eighty pounds and four ounces.
Such quantities, it is certain, could not be supplied by
any possible amount of meat and drink consumed within
the time specified. It is the same blood, consequently,
that is now flowing out by the arteries, now returning by
the veins; and it is simply matter of necessity that
the blood should perform a circuit, or return to the place
from whence it went forth."

Demonstration of the second proposition—that the
blood enters a limb by the arteries and returns from it
by the veins—is afforded by the effects of a ligature.
For if the upper part of the arm be *tightly* bound, the
arteries below will not pulsate, while those above will
throb violently. The hand under such circumstances
will retain its natural colour and appearance, although, if
the bandage be kept on for a minute or two, it will
begin to look livid and to fall in temperature. But
if the bandage be now slackened a little, the hand and
the arm will immediately become suffused, and the super-

ficial veins show themselves tumid and knotted, the pulse at the wrist in the same instant beginning to beat as it did before the application of the bandage. The tight bandage not only compresses the veins, but the arteries also, so that blood cannot flow through either. The slacker ligature obstructs the veins only, for the arteries lie deeper and have firmer coats. "Seeing, then," says Harvey, "that the moderately tight ligature renders the veins turgid, and the whole hand full of blood, I ask, Whence is this? Does the blood accumulate below the ligature coming through the veins, or through the arteries, or passing by certain secret pores? Through the veins it cannot come; still less can it come by any system of invisible pores; it must needs, then, arrive by the arteries."

The third position to be proved is that the veins return the blood to the heart from all parts of the body. That such is the case might be inferred from the presence and disposition of the valves in the veins; for the office of the valves is by no means explained by the theory that they are to hinder the blood from flowing into inferior parts by gravitation, since the valves do not always look upwards, but always towards the trunks of the veins, invariably towards the seat of the heart. The action of the valves is then demonstrated experimentally on the arm bound as for blood-letting. The point of a finger being kept on a vein, the blood from the space above may be streaked upwards till it passes the valve, when that portion of the vein between the valve and the point of pressure will not only be emptied of its contents, but will remain empty as long as the pressure is continued. If the pressure be now removed, the empty part of the vein will fill instantly and look as turgid as before.

Other confirmatory evidence is then added, *e.g.* the absorption of animal poisons and of medicines applied externally, the muscular structure of the heart and the necessary working of its valves.

William Harvey, the illustrious physiologist, anatomist, and physician, to whom this discovery is due, was the eldest son of a Kentish yeoman, and was born in April, 1578. At the age of ten he entered the Canterbury Grammar School, where he appears to have remained for some years. At sixteen he passed to Caius-Gonvil College, Cambridge, and three years afterwards took his B.A. degree and quitted the university. Like most students of medicine of that day, he found it necessary to seek the principal part of his professional education abroad. He travelled to Italy, selected Padua as his place of study, and there continued to reside for four years, having as one of his teachers the famous Fabricius of Aquapendente. On his return to England, in 1602, he took his doctor's degree at Cambridge, and entered on the practice of his profession.

In 1604 he joined the College of Physicians, and three years later was elected a Fellow of that learned body. Two years afterwards he applied for the post of physician to St. Bartholomew's Hospital ; and his application being supported by letters of recommendation to the governor, from the king and from the president of the College of Physicians, he was duly elected to the office in the same year, as soon as a vacancy occurred.

In 1615, when thirty-seven years of age, Harvey was chosen to deliver the lectures on surgery and anatomy to the College of Physicians, and it is possible that at this time he gave an exposition of his views on the circulation. He continued to lecture on the same subject for many years afterwards, although he did not publish his views until 1628, when they appeared in the work "De Motu Cordis."

Some few years after his appointment as lecturer to the college, he was chosen one of the physicians extraordinary to King James I., and about five or six years after the accession of Charles I. he became physician in ordinary to that unfortunate monarch. The physiologist's investigations seem to have interested King Charles, for he had several exhibitions made of the *punctum saliens* in the embryo chick, and also witnessed dissections from time to time.

When, in 1630, the young Duke of Lennox made a journey on the Continent, Harvey was chosen to travel with him, and probably remained abroad about two years. During this time Harvey most likely visited Venice. Of this tour the doctor speaks in the following terms in a letter written at the time : " I can only complayne that by the waye we could scarce see a dogg, crow, kite, raven, or any bird or any thing to anatomise ; only sum few miserable poeple the reliques of the war and the plauge, where famine had made anatomies before I came."

Six years after this, in April, 1636, he accompanied the Earl of Arundel in his embassy to the emperor. Having to visit the principal cities of Germany, he was thus afforded an opportunity of meeting the leading biologists of the time, and at Nuremberg he probably met Caspar Hoffmann, and made that public demonstration of the circulation of the blood which he had promised in his letter dated from that city, and which convinced every one present except Hoffmann himself. Hollar, the artist, informs us that Harvey's enthusiasm in his search for specimens often led him into danger, and caused grave anxiety to the Earl of Arundel. " For he would still be making of excursions into the woods, making observations of strange trees, plants, earths, etc., and sometimes like to be lost ; so that my lord ambassador would be really angry with him, for there was not only danger of wild beasts, but of thieves."

Soon after his return to England, as court physician, his movements became seriously restricted by the

fortunes of the king. Aubrey says, "When King
Charles I., by reason of the tumults, left London, Harvey
attended him, and was at the fight of Edgehill with him ;
and during the fight the Prince and the Duke of York
were committed to his care. He told me that he with-
drew with them under a hedge, and tooke out of his
pockett a booke and read ; but he had not read very
long before a bullet of a great gun grazed on the ground
neare him, which made him remove his station. . . .
I first sawe him at Oxford, 1642, after Edgehill fight,
but was then too young to be acquainted with so great
a doctor. I remember he came severall times to our
Coll. (Trin.) to George Bathurst, B.D., who had a
hen to hatch egges in his chamber, which they dayly
opened to see the progress and way of generation."

In 1645, Charles, after the execution of Archbishop
Laud, took upon himself the functions of visitor of
Merton College, and having removed Sir Nathaniel
Brent from the office of warden for having joined "the
Rebells now in armes against" him, he directed the
Fellows to take the necessary steps for the election of
a successor. This course consisted in giving in three
names to the visitor, in order that one of the three (the
one named first, probably) should be appointed. Harvey
was so named by five out of the seven Fellows voting,
and was accordingly duly elected. A couple of days
after his admission he summoned the Fellows into the

hall and made a speech to them, in which he pointed
out that it was likely enough that some of his predecessors
had sought the office in order to enrich themselves, but
that his intentions were quite of another kind, wishing as
he did to increase the wealth and prosperity of the
college; and he finished by exhorting them to cherish
mutual concord and amity. After the surrender of
Oxford, July, 1646, Harvey retired from the court. He
was in his sixty-ninth year, and doubtless found the
hardships and inconveniences which the miserable war
entailed far from conducive to health. The rest and
seclusion to be had at the residence of one or other of
his brothers offered him the much-needed opportunity of
renewing his inquiries into the subject of generation, and
it is of this time that Dr. Ent speaks in the preface to
the published work on that subject which appeared in
1651. "Harassed with anxious and in the end not
much availing cares, about Christmas last, I sought to
rid my spirit of the cloud that oppressed it, by a visit to
that great man, the chief honour and ornament of our
college, Dr. William Harvey, then dwelling not far from
the city. I found him, Democritus-like, busy with the
study of natural things, his countenance cheerful, his
mind serene, embracing all within its sphere. I forthwith
saluted him, and asked if all were well with him. 'How
can it,' said he, 'whilst the Commonwealth is full of
distractions, and I myself am still in the open sea? And

truly,' he continued, 'did I not find solace in my studies, and a balm for my spirit in the memory of my observations of former years, I should feel little desire for longer life. But so it has been, that this life of obscurity, this vacation from public business, which causes tedium and disgust to so many, has proved a sovereign remedy to me.'"

Harvey died in June, 1657. Aubrey, his contemporary, says, "On the morning of his death, about ten o'clock, he went to speake, and found he had the dead palsey in his tongue; then he sawe what was to become of him, he knew there was then no hopes of his recovery, so presently sends for his young nephews to come up to him, to whom he gives one his watch, to another another remembrance, etc.; made sign to Sambroke his Apothecary to lett him blood in the tongue, which did little or no good, and so he ended his dayes. . . . The palsey did give him an easie passeport. . . . He lies buried in a vault at Hempsted in Essex, which his brother Eliab Harvey built; he is lapt in lead, and on his brest, in great letters, 'Dr. William Harvey.' I was at his Funerall, and helpt to carry him into the vault."

The publication of Harvey's views on the movement of the blood excited great surprise and opposition. The theory of a complete circulation was at any rate novel, but novelty was far from being a recommendation in those days. According to Aubrey, the author was thought to be crackbrained, and lost much of his practice in consequence. He himself complains that contumelious epithets were levelled at the doctrine and its author. It was not until after many years had elapsed, and the facts had become familiar, that men were struck with the simplicity of the theory, and tried to prove that the idea was not new after all, and that it was to be found in Hippocrates, or in Galen, or in Servetus, or in Cæsalpinus—anywhere, in fact, except where alone it existed, namely, in the work, "De Motu Cordis et Sanguinis." No one seems to have denied, while Harvey lived, that he was the discoverer of the circulation of the blood; indeed, Hobbes of Malmesbury, his contemporary, said of him, " He is the only man, perhaps, that ever lived to see his own doctrine established in his lifetime."

In one important respect Harvey's account of the circulation was incomplete. He knew nothing of the vessels which we now speak of as capillaries. Writing to Paul Marquard Slegel, of Hamburg, in 1651, he says, "When I perceived that the blood is transferred from the veins into the arteries through the medium of the heart, by a grand mechanism and exquisite apparatus of valves, I judged that in like manner, wherever transudation does not take place through the pores of the flesh, the blood is returned from the arteries to the veins, not without some other admirable artifice" (*non sine artificio quodam admirabili*). It was this *artificium admirabile* of which Harvey was unable to give a description. On account of the minuteness of their structure, the capillaries were beyond his sight, aided as it was by a magnifying glass merely. He indeed demonstrated physiologically the existence of some such passages; but it remained for a later observer, with improved appliances, to verify the fact. This was done by Malpighi in 1661, who saw in the lung of a frog, which was so mounted in a frame as to be viewed by transmitted light, the network of capillaries which connect the last ramifications of the arteries with the radicles of the veins.

Harvey rightly denied that the arteries possessed any pulsific power of their own, and maintained that their pulse is owing solely to the sudden distension of their walls by the blood thrown into them at each contraction of the ventricles. But the remission which succeeds the pulse was regarded by him as caused simply by collapse of the walls of the arteries due to elastic reaction. Knowing nothing of the muscular coat of the arteries, he was unaware of the fact that the elastic reaction of the arteries, after their distension, is aided by the tonic contractility of their walls; the two forces, physical and vital, acting in concert with each other— the former converting the intermittent flow from the heart into an even stream in the capillaries and veins;

the latter, through the vaso motor system, regulating the flow of blood to particular parts in order to meet changing requirements.

It is somewhat surprising to find that such an accurate observer as Harvey should have failed to recognize the significance and importance of the system of lacteal vessels. But such was the case. Eustachius, in the sixteenth century, had discovered the thoracic duct in the horse, although he seems to have thought that it was peculiar to that animal. Aselli, while dissecting the body of a dog in 1622, accidentally discovered the lacteals, and thought at first that they were nerves; but upon puncturing one of them, and seeing the milky fluid which escaped, found them to be vessels. He, however, failed to trace them to the thoracic duct, and believed them to terminate in the liver. Pecquet of Dieppe followed them from the intestines to the mesenteric glands, and from these into a common sac or reservoir, which he designated *receptaculum chyli*, and thence to their entry by a single slender conduit into the venous system at the junction of the jugular and subclavian veins. The existence of the lacteals had not entirely escaped Harvey, however. He had himself noticed them in the course of his dissections before Aselli's book was published, but "for various reasons" could not bring himself to believe that they contained chyle. The smallness of the thoracic duct seemed to him a difficulty, and as it was a demonstrated fact that the gastric veins were largely absorptive, the lacteals appeared to him super-fluous. He is not "obstinately wedded to his own opinion," and does not doubt "but that many things, now hidden in the well of Democritus, will by-and-by be drawn up into day by the ceaseless industry of a coming age."

Late in the author's life, as we have seen, the work on the "Generation of Animals" appeared; but neither physiological nor microscopical science was sufficiently advanced to admit of the production of an enduring work on a subject necessarily so abstruse as that of generation. It was impossible, however, for so shrewd and able an investigator as Harvey to work at a subject even as difficult as this without leaving the impress of his original genius. He first announced the general truth, "Omne animal ex ovo," and clearly proved that the essential part of the egg, that in which the repro-ductive processes begin, was not the *chalazæ*, but the *cicatricula*. This Fabricius had looked upon as a blemish, a scar left by a broken peduncle. Harvey described this little cicatricula as expanding under the influence of incubation into a wider structure, which he called the eye of the egg, and at the same time separating into a clear and transparent part, in which later on, according to him, there appeared, as the first rudiment of the embryo, the heart, or *punctum saliens*, together with the blood-vessels. He was clearly of opinion that the embryo arose by successive formation of parts out of the homogeneous and nearly liquid mass. This was the doctrine of epigenesis, which, notwithstanding its temporary overthrow by the erroneous theory of evolution,[1] is, with modifications, the doctrine now held.

Of Harvey's scholarship and culture we are not left in ignorance. Bishop Pearson, writing about seven years after the doctor's death, and Aubrey[2] have told us of his appreciation of the works of Aristotle, and in his own writings he refers more frequently to the Stagirite than to any other individual. Sir William Temple[3] has also put it on record that the famous Dr. Harvey was a great admirer of Virgil, whose works were frequently in his hands. His store of individual knowledge must have been great; and he seems never to have flagged in his anxiety to learn more. He made himself master of Oughtred's " Clavis Mathematica " in his old age, according to Aubrey, who found him " perusing it and working problems not long before he dyed."

Nor should it be forgotten that this illustrious physiolo-

---

[1] According to the theory of evolution, the egg contained from the first an excessively minute, but complete animal, and the changes which took place during incubation consisted not in a formation of parts, but in a growth, *i.e.* in an expansion of the already existing embryo (see p. 40).

[2] See p. lxxxii. of " Life," by Dr. Willis.

[3] " Miscellanies : " Part II. on Poetry, p. 314.

gist and scholar was also the first English comparative anatomist. Of his knowledge of the lower animals he makes frequent use, and he says (in his work on the heart), " Had anatomists only been as conversant with the dissection of the lower animals as they are with that of the human body, many matters that have hitherto kept them in a perplexity of doubt, would, in my opinion, have met them freed from every kind of difficulty." Aubrey says that Harvey often told him " that of all the losses he sustained, no grief was so crucifying to him as the loss of his papers (containing notes of his dissections of the frog, toad, and other animals), which, together with his goods in his lodgings at Whitehall, were plundered at the beginning of the rebellion."

INDEX.

Albertus Magnus, 65
Alexander the Great, 23, 24
Andronicus of Rhodes, 27
" Animals, History of," by Aristotle, 27
" Animals, On the Parts of," by Aristotle, 31
Antipater, Governor of Macedonia, 25
Apellicon, 27
"Aphorisms" of Hippocrates, 12
Aristotle, birth, 21 ; youth, 22 ; zoological researches, 24 ; charge against, 25 ; death, 26 ; history of the manuscripts of his works, 26 ; account of his biological writings, 27-44 ; his philosophy,of nature teleological, 39
Arundel, Earl of, 94
Asclepiads, physical training among the, 4
Asclepions, description of the, 4
Aselli, 100
Aubrey, 95, 97, 98, 102

Bathurst, George, 95
Blood, description of, by Aristotle, 31

Blood, opinions before the time of Harvey as to the movements of the, 85, 86
Bogarucci, 76
Brain, description of the, by Aristotle, 33
Browne, Sir Thomas, 65

Cæsalpinus, 98
Calcar, Jean, 71
Callisthenes, 24
Capillaries, discovery of the, 99
" Corporis Humani Fabrica," 72
Cuvier's exaggerated praise of Aristotle, 41

" Dead image of God," the, 65
" De Anatome," 66
"De Motu Cordis et Sanguinis," 88-92
" De usu Radicis, Chinæ," 73
Disease, causes of, 7
" Disease, The Sacred," 6
Diseases, natural history of, 9
Dissection of the human body, 10, 52
" Divine old man," the, 3

Don Carlos, cure of, 75
Ductus venosus, observed by Vesalius, 79

Ent, Dr., 96
" Epigenesis " and " evolution " compared, 40, 102
Etienne's observation confirmed by Vesalius, 79
Erasistratus, 47, 58, 85
Eustachius, discovery of the thoracic duct of the horse by, 100

Fabricius of Aquapendente, 85, 92
Fallopius, anatomical observations of, 77
" Father of medicine," the, 3
Franciscus Puteus, reply to, by Gabriel Cuneus, 77
Foramen ovale, valve guarding the, 79

Galen, birth, 48 ; influence, 49, 60, 65 ; education, 49 ; at Smyrna, 49 ; at Alexandria, 49 ; at Pergamus, 50 ; at Rome, 50 ; return to Greece, 50 ; summoned to meet the Emperors at Aquileia, 50 ; death, 51 ; writings, 51 ; views as to the modes of existence, 52 ; and osteology, 53 ; and the nervous system, 53 ; and the lacteals, 54 ; the heart, 55 ; the arteries, 56 ; and respiration, 57–59 ; made a

near approach to the Harveian theory of the circulation, 57
Generation of animals, the, 38, 101
Geynes, Dr., 60

Harvey, date and place of birth, 92 ; at Canterbury School, 92 ; at Cambridge, 92 ; at Padua, 92 ; elected Fellow of the College of Physicians, 93 ; appointed physician to St. Bartholomew's Hospital, 93 ; physician to Charles I., 93 ; foreign travels, 94 ; present at the battle of Edgehill, 95 ; elected Warden of Merton College, 95 ; death, 97 ; discovery of the circulation incomplete in one respect, 98, 99 ; work on the generation of animals, 101 ; a scholar, 102 ; and comparative anatomist, 103
Heart, description of the, by Aristotle, 35
Hellebore, administered by Hippocrates, 9
Hermias despot of Atarneus, 22 ; murder of, 23
Herophilus, 47, 58, 85
Hippocrates, date of birth, 3 ; Greek contemporaries, 3 ; birthplace, 3 ; his freedom from superstition, 5, 16 ; compared with Socrates, 7 ; medical doctrines of, 8 ; works, 10 ; knowledge of osteology,

10; traditions concerning, 14; oath of, 16
Hobbes of Malmesbury, 98
Hoffmann, Caspar, 94
Humours, the four, 8
Huxley, Professor, on errors attributed to Aristotle, 37, 42

Lacteals, the, 54, 100
Lennox, Duke of, 93
Lungs, Aristotle's description of the, 37

Malpighi, discovery of the capillaries by, 99
Marcus Aurelius, 50
Marine animals, description of, by Aristotle, 29
Mediastinum, correct description of the, by Vesalius, 79
Milk in male animals, occasional appearance of, 29
Mundinus, 66

Neleus, 26
Nicon, father of Galen, 49

Omentum, the, and its connections, 80
Owen, Professor, on Aristotle's knowledge of the cephalopoda, 29

" Parva naturalia," 27
Pausanias, 15
Pecquet of Dieppe, 100
Peripatetics, the, 24

Philip, father of Alexander, 22, 23
" Physiological division of labour," 43
Plato, 22
Pliny, 47, 48
Pneuma, 38
Punctum saliens, 35, 93, 101
Pylorus, the, described by Vesalius, 80
Pythias, 23

Receptaculum chyli, 100
Roelants, Joachim, 78

Scamnum Hippocratis, 12
Servetus, 86
Septimius Severus, 51
Slegel of Hamburg, 98
Socrates compared with Hippocrates, 7
Sprengel's opinion of Galen, 60
Sylla, 27
Sylvius, 67, 72, 73, 74

Teupulus, Paulus, 77
Theophrastus, 26
Theriac, the, 50
Thoracic duct, discovery of, 100
Tyrannion, 27

Vesalius, birth, 66 ; scholarship, 66; studied under Sylvius, 67 ; and Winter of Andernach, 67 ; adventure at Louvain, 67, 68 ; appointed professor at Padua, at Bologna, and at Pisa, 69; zeal for correctness in anatomy, 70; skill in diagnosis, 70; distrusts infallibility of Galen's teaching, 71; writes "Fabric of the Human Body," 72; is summoned to Ratisbon, 73; destroys his manuscripts, 74; his success as a practitioner, 75; charged with impiety, 75; is sent on pilgrimage, 75; shipwreck and death at Zante, 76; works, 76–80

Vix medicatrix naturæ, 9

Winter of Andernach, 67

www.ingramcontent.com/pod-product-compliance
Lightning Source LLC
Chambersburg PA
CBHW032110010726
47493CB00008B/2530